Introducing Murdo

The Battle Collection

Four Short Stories – Inspired by Robert Burns Poems

To CARLY, ANDREW & BRADLEY
MAY THE FORCE OF ROBERT BURNS
BE WITH YOU.

Norman Thomson
2015

Written by   Norman Thomson
Illustrated by   Nicholas Lennox

Date of Registration April 10th 2014
Registration Number 1112359

Published by
Norman Thomson

Canadian Cataloguing in Publication Data

Thomson, Norman

Introducing Mr. B. -- The Battle Collection

ISBN 978-0-9936127-8-7

Illustrated by Nicholas Lennox

Contents

The Original Poems by Robert Burns.
(With embedded interpretations)

Dedicated to our sons Mark and Scott

This Lion Roars

From Robert Burns' poem

Caledonia

"Whoe're shall provoke thee, th' encounter shall rue!"

The school bus pulled into the parking lot beside the geodesic dome of Science World. Ms. Cormier was the teacher in charge and held up her hand to indicate she wanted the students to be quiet.

"The main reason we're here today is to see a special exhibit on the history and independence of Scotland," she said. "We've reserved a block of seats on the people mover that'll take you through this display and we'll be finished before it opens to the general public. After we've seen it you'll have one hour to visit some of the other displays and then you must report to the cafeteria where we'll assemble before boarding the bus. 'Everybody understand that? Any questions? Okay, let's go."

The students had to get into pairs to sit on the people mover, and Astrid and Simone made sure they went together.

Once they
were seated they
put on the
headphones and
listened to an audio track explaining about the displays
they were going to see.

The first room that they came to had a large map
of Scotland. The audio told them that in the beginning
what would become Scotland started at the river Tweed
and went to John o' Groats at the Northern most tip.
While there was no border between Scotland and
England, the Scottish people spoke Gaelic and this
separated them from the English speaking southerners.
Relative to today there was quite a small population in
Scotland, so there was plenty of land to grow crops and
raise sheep to feed and clothe everyone. But it wasn't a
peaceful place. There were many different clans and they
often fought amongst themselves. This was probably how
they honed the fighting skills that defeated invaders, who
came to regret attacking this country.

Astrid poked Simone and asked, "What clan are your family from?"

"I think we're part of the Campbells; my dad has one of their kilts. There's no doubt about your clan with your family name of McLeod," said Simone.

"Yes, we went on holiday to Skye where the clan castle is," said Astrid. "But my grandmother told me my name, Astrid, is from Norway or Sweden."

The next room that the people mover brought them into had several pictures of the Roman Empire that needed an encompassing map of Europe. The audio track informed them that Roman Legions had fanned out from Rome, conquered Europe and sailed across the channel. Here they battled and beat the English and started to build the city of London about the year AD 50. Ambitious as always, the Romans built roads and bridges to the north so they could quickly move their army to control these regions. When they reached that undefined border of the River Tweed they were taken by surprise. The Scottish clansmen lost a battle with the Romans, but unlike other countries, the surviving Scottish recognized that they couldn't fight the well-armed Roman soldiers in the battlefield. They developed the use of what we now call guerrilla tactics. The Scots took to the hills and ambushed groups of the Romans when they were not prepared for battle.

The Roman generals could see that their army, with all its armour and shields, couldn't move quickly enough through the forests and heather clad hills to catch the Scots. Wisely, the Romans decided to retreat, and built two massive walls to try and keep the Scots from coming to fight them in England. Hadrian's Wall was built from the Solway Firth in the west to the river Tyne in the east.

Later, a second wall, Antonine's Wall, was built on the land joining the Firth of Clyde to the Firth of Forth. The Romans stayed on the south of these walls and never ruled Scotland. The country's independence

had survived this first major challenge.

Simone said, "You can still see parts of Hadrian's wall. When we were going to England my dad stopped and we all went and hiked along part of it."

"Was it big like the great wall of China?" Astrid asked.

"No, not that big. Nearly all you can see now are the stone foundations, which are overgrown with grass. But my dad said they had lots of forts along the wall to keep the Scots from coming to England."

Once more the people mover brought the students into another room and this time the main map focused on Scandinavia. "You are now entering the time zone about AD 1000, when King Kenneth the third was Scotland's King," the audio voice narrated. This time it was the Danes who tried to invade Scotland. They landed where the seaside town of Montrose is today. When the Danes came ashore with their army they brutally slaughtered and burned the coastal towns. They did the same as they made their way inland along the river Tay and took the town of Perth.

King Kenneth raised an army of Scots, who marched from Stirling to battle the Danes. The King set up his army outside Perth in the lands adjoining the village of Luncarty. A great battle ensued, and at first the Scots had the advantage, but then the Danes counter-attacked and the Scots' army fled in retreat.

Then a very strange thing happened. Nearby a farmer, whose name was Hay saw the Scots running away from the battle and he was mad at the humiliation this would cause. He called his two sons to get their swords and follow him. They knew the retreating soldiers would have to pass through a narrow gap in the rocky hillside. Quickly they positioned themselves there and when the soldiers appeared Hay and his sons roared and attacked their own Scottish soldiers. Confusion reigned.

The Scots' soldiers believed the farmer and his sons were Danes, and decided to turn around and fight the Danish soldiers who were pursing them. Now the Danes believed that new reinforcements had arrived for the Scots and they dropped their weapons so they could run faster to escape. Charging ahead, the Scots including the Hay family routed the Danes. The Scots had succeeded in repelling this second challenge to their independence.

Simone said, "My granddad was born in Perth. When we visited there we went to the Black Watch army museum."

"Did they fight the Danes?" Astrid asked.

"No, the army isn't that old."

"A third invasion of Scotland came from the Vikings of Norway," the audio continued.

Trouble arose between the two countries after the Scots' King Alexander the third had tried to buy the Outer Hebrides and other islands, which were controlled by the Norwegians. The negotiations failed and when a

Scottish earl started raiding the Isle of Skye, the Viking King Haakon responded by assembling a fleet of ships to bring his army to defend the islands. In those days it was a massive fleet of about one hundred and twenty ships filled with soldiers. The battle lines were drawn near the town of Largs on the Ayrshire coast. King Haakon anchored his fleet off the island of Arran, while the Scottish army was positioned on the hills surrounding the bay at Largs and prepared for a battle.

The Scots initially sent messengers out in boats to meet the Vikings, to see if they could negotiate a peace treaty; but the talks dragged on for more than a month without any resolution. In an effort to intimidate the Scots, the Viking fleet moved closer to the mainland and anchored again. This turned out to be a poor choice when a storm arose and blasted through their fleet, driving some of the ships ashore. With these Viking crews in a state of disarray, the Scots took advantage and attacked.

The battle carried on the next day when some of the other Vikings came ashore to rescue their boats and trapped comrades. But the Scots fought hard and forced the Vikings to retreat in panic. As they scrambled to get onboard, some of their boats capsized. The battle raged along the shore until the Vikings limped back to what was left of their fleet. The Scots hailed it as a great victory as they watched the Viking armada sail in retreat out of the Firth of Clyde.

King Haakon was determined to return to the battle and sailed his fleet to the Orkney Islands. His plan was to give his army time to regroup, repair some ships and return again in the spring to resume the battle. But on December 15, 1263, King Haakon became ill and died.

The Vikings sailed back to Norway rather than return to fight the Scots. The third challenge to Scotland's independence had been defeated. Two years later an agreement for the sale of the Hebrides and other islands to Scotland was concluded. A document recorded the terms of the agreement in the Treaty of Perth 1266. Scotland had remained independent from these two Scandinavian challengers.

Simone nudged Astrid. "You said your name was Norwegian."

"Yes, that's what my grandmother told me," said Astrid.

"Well you're our enemy then," said Simone.

"Like, I don't think so. It's just a name. Simone sounds French; are you French?"

"No, I'm Scottish."

"So am I."

The audio system took over saying that the last challenge to Scotland's independence came from the English, who were her main adversary. A series of battles that became known as the Wars of Independence raged

between Scotland and England for more than a century. One of the earliest battles was in 1297, when the Scots' hero, William Wallace, defeated the English at the battle of Stirling Bridge.

There were many battles with wins and losses on both sides. The true measure occurred later, when in 1603, both countries came together under the reign of King James the sixth of Scotland. King James was asked to become the King of England and the two countries united to become the Kingdom of Great Britain.

The audio said this was the end of the presentation on how Scotland always managed to maintain its independence. The people mover came to a stop in the same room as it had started, and Simone and Astrid took off the earphones and stepped out the car.

"Come on and look at some of the other exhibits before we have to leave," said Simone.

"Yes, they've got one on how they make special effects in movies. Let's try and find that one," said Astrid. They did find it and had fun posing in front of a green screen where a camera took images of them. These were projected onto a screen that set them in a James Bond movie scene, clinging to the cables of the Golden Gate Bridge in San Francisco. They were having a great time when they dropped to the floor and on the screen it looked as though they fell from the cables. That hour they were allowed must have passed quickly, because suddenly over the intercom came a tinny voice demanding that Astrid and Simone return to the cafeteria immediately. When they got there Ms. Cormier was initially relieved to see them and then told them to get on the bus right away, as everyone else had returned on time.

Devils and Witches

From Robert Burns' poem

Tam O'Shanter

"Now, do thy speedy utmost, Meg,
And win the key-stane of the brig:
There, at them thou thy tail may toss,
A running stream they dare na cross!"

Davy couldn't wait to get back from school and try out his present from his grandmother. It was his private time between getting home and before his parents arrived back from work. He dropped his school bag on the floor as he came through the kitchen door and grabbed an apple out the fruit basket. Davy was tall for his age, with blond tints in his dark, brown, spiky hair. His fourteenth birthday was last month and the present was a game: "The Devil and Tam O'Shanter."

The cover had a grizzly picture on the front and Davy had already torn open the package to read the instructions. He knew his parents would want him to be working on his homework, but that would have to wait while he tried out the game. In the family room he clicked the remote to put on the TV, powered up the Wii system and loaded the game disc. With the controls in his hands he perched himself on the edge of the sofa.

A picture of the devil filled the screen and then faded to show an attractive woman sitting in her cottage. A subtitle said she was Kate O'Shanter in her cottage in

Alloway in Ayrshire and the year was 1780. She was
nervously chewing on a loose strand of her red hair as
she looked out the window for her husband.

The screen filled with an aerial sweep from the
cottage door over the countryside, along rivers, past
forests, following tracks in fields with gates and stiles.
Then the scene switched to show a party in a tavern. A
close up shot picked out one of the tables, where a group
of men were singing and drinking.

The camera focused in on one of the
revellers – Tam O'Shanter. Davy saw
Tam had a pot-belly that overhung
the belt on his trousers. Still, he
radiated a happy smile on his red,
flushed face that was crowned with a
head of dark, curly hair. He pulled
the chain on his pocket watch and flipped open the case
to check the time.

A voice-over played Kate's voice saying, "If you
keep partying too much you'll end up falling off your

horse into the river Doon, or worse being caught by witches at the haunted church.

The game controls became *active in Davy's hands* and he made Tam wave farewell to his partying friends, turn around and step out of the tavern door into a black, stormy night. The wind blew, lightning flashed, thunder roared and the rain poured down. *With the control stick, Davy* walked Tam to the stables to get his horse, called Meg, and when *Davy pressed the control button* Tam mounted his horse. *Davy gently tilted the control stick forward and* moved them out of the stable and on the screen it showed a road stretching out into the dark night. *Skilfully, Davy made* them ride fast, following the road's twist and turns. Tam held on to his blue cap so that it didn't get blown away. He sang a few lines from some of the songs he had been singing in the tavern and checked over his shoulder to make sure nothing was chasing him.

The road swept down a hill to a normally shallow crossing on the river Doon. But on this night the river was running like a torrent, with the water crashing against the rocks and spray flying into the air, mixing with the torrential rain. ***Davy pulled back the control stick*** and stopped Meg by the river. Boulders came crashing through the water but he knew they had to cross over here. ***Delicately, Davy moved the stick*** and Meg slowly ventured into the river. Suddenly, a rock came blasting towards them and ***Davy quickly shook the stick,*** which made Meg jump straight up, so that the rock passed as Meg landed back in the river. ***Again, with a soft touch, Davy slowly and cautiously*** made Meg continue to cross the raging river. Crack! An overhead tree broke loose and fell. It was swept towards them and ***Davy pressed the controller's red button,*** **which** made Meg leap, just in time, to the river's edge. The tree pitched and tossed wildly past.

    Davy pressed the controller's green button and checked Tam's health status. It showed he was in good shape to keep going. Then the screen displayed three challenges and Davy had to pick one. They were:

- Find your way past the birch trees and big rocks to where Charley broke his neck.

- Ride through the bracken to the memorial marker where hunters found the body of a child killed in an accident.
- Take the path to the wishing well where Mungo's mother drowned.

Davy chose number three. The screen showed a twisted path disappearing into the forest. *Now he moved the control stick* and Tam, on Meg, moved forward. Only when bolts of lightning flashed could the way ahead be seen. At last they came to a clearing, with a wishing well in the middle. A message on the screen offered a challenge. Toss a coin in the well and choose from one of two boxes shown on the screen. *Davy pressed the green button to accept the challenge.* Tam removed a coin from his pouch and pitched it into the well. The screen lit up and *Davy picked* one of the boxes. A message appeared on the screen, "Take the bottle of courage potion and the shortcut home." The screen had four paths leading out the clearing and one of them now had an arrow saying "Shortcut ." *Davy made* Tam and Meg start down this path through the woods. The storm still raged, and forked and sheet lightning filled the sky, but Tam persevered and continued through the forest. A source of new lights flashed  through the trees ominously and they were not coming from the lightning. As Tam approached the Church of Alloway it was completely flooded with light, as though the whole place was ablaze. Loud bagpipe music filled the air and mingled with sounds of people dancing and laughing.

Davy again checked Tam's health status, as he recognised that the scene was likely to put Tam in a dangerous situation. The screen said all was still well; down a bit – but still safe.

Davy opened Tam's inventory screen and selected the courage potion. Tam drank it and said, "Man I feel great; I wouldn't even be afraid to meet the devil tonight."

But he hadn't made Meg drink any, and when he wanted her to move forward she just dug in her hoofs and stood still. Tam had to slap her and drive in his spurs before she slowly moved forward. ***Davy stopped them*** at the edge of the forest. The music was getting louder. ***Davy made*** Tam come down off Meg and inch forward, lying on his stomach, till he looked into the graveyard. And, wow! He saw an incredible sight!

Davy knew that a cut scene had taken over and he rested his hands on the controls while this played out. It showed the graveyard was alive with warlocks and witches who danced wildly. Tam's eyes were wide open as he watched them cavorting through Scottish reels and jigs.

Then his heart just about stopped when his eyes were drawn to one of the church windows. There sat the Devil in the guise of a horrific beast. It had a body twice the size of any man's, covered in thick black hair. The head was an evil wolf, from which its red luminous eyes pierced the night like laser beams. He was making strange music with bagpipes; an unearthly, screeching sound that made the church windows rattle as though they would shatter at any moment.

A cold sweat broke out on Tam's forehead as he looked around the edge of the graveyard. All around coffins stood upright and in each there was either a skeleton or a dead body in a funeral dress. These corpses all held in their bony hands a bright candlelight that shone on the dancers below. In front of the devil was the holy table from the church, strewn with a grizzly collection of the instruments of death. Tam was mesmerized. If possible, the dancing became even faster and wilder following the tempo of the music. The witches and warlocks had sweat pouring off them.

You had to wonder why anybody would watch as closely as Tam. The witches were old and their clothes were greasy. But there was one pretty witch and she stood out in the coven. Those that knew her were afraid of her powers. With her pretty looks, like a siren, she had lured boats to crash on the rocks and she killed lots of animals. She was wearing a short, paisley-patterned skirt that her grandmother had given her when she was a wee girl called Nannie

Tam was watching only her now. She danced and leapt and kicked her heels in the air as though she was possessed of magical powers. If Tam could have taken his eyes off her he would have seen that even the devil was hypnotized by Nannie's dancing. Without thinking, Tam broke the spell when he suddenly roared out loud "Well done short skirt!"

In an instant the screen went black, and ***Davy knew the cut scene was over and he tightened his hands on the controller.*** The screen came alive again and all the witches and warlocks were racing towards Tam. ***Davy made*** Tam run back and mount his horse. There was no getting back into the game slowly; Tam and Meg had to go as fast as they could. Tam looked over his shoulder and saw the swarm of witches and warlocks racing after him like bees charging out of a hive. A message appeared on the screen: "The horseman must make it over the middle of the bridge because witches cannot cross a running river."

Davy had to move the stick left and right quickly; this made Tam and Meg safely follow the twists and turns through the forest path. When a fallen tree was over the path ***Davy had to keep the stick forward and pressed the flip button.*** Meg jumped over the log and stayed running flat out. A low, stone wall appeared on the screen, and ***again Davy flipped the button*** and Meg jumped – but she only just managed to clear as her hooves clacked on the top stones. The witches floated over the ground and Nannie was in the lead, closing the gap between her and Meg. Tam could be heard to say breathlessly to himself, "If they catch me they'll roast me alive." The screen overlaid a thought bubble that showed Kate. Again Tam's desperate voice was heard saying, "If I die tonight Kate'll be really sad." Tam drove his spurs into Meg's side when he saw the bridge just ahead of him. But he heard an awful laugh as Nannie reached out and grabbed Meg's tail and she started to slow.

Tam's spurs drove into Meg's side and blood appeared on her fur. ***Davy hit the control stick*** and made Meg take one giant lurch and they crossed the middle point of the bridge. Nannie immediately stopped in midair and Meg's tail was ripped off.

Davy pressed the yellow and green buttons and Tam dismounted from Meg. He patted her head and thanked her for saving him. Then he walked to look at her poor tail's stump. ***Davy laughed and wondered what would happen next time if Nannie caught them.***

Devils and Witches

Two Mountain Bikers

From Robert Burns' poem

The Twa Dogs

"An' each took aff his several way

Resolv'd to meet some ither day."

"Caesar." It was a terrible name to have. Kids made puns of it, saying "seize her," or they stuck their arm in the air, "all hail Caesar." He was used to it now and luckily he was bigger than most boys his age and stronger so when he told them to "lay off," they did. Caesar had to learn to be strong early in life, when his mother and father's fishing boat sank off the coast of Newfoundland and they drowned. His uncle, who lived in Coilsfield mansion house in Ayrshire, adopted Caesar.

There wasn't anything his uncle wouldn't do for Caesar and when he asked for a mountain bike his uncle bought a top of the line bike. It had front and rear shocks, a full range of gears and a frame made from lightweight titanium. To make sure it didn't get lost or stolen his uncle had engraved identification marks on the frame and a GPS tracking chip attached.

Because Caesar was self-conscious about his name it was almost automatic that he was drawn to become friends with another boy at school with an equally unusual name. His name was Luath, and while he was smaller than Caesar he was wiry and strong from working on his father's farm. When Caesar asked him where his name came from, he said his father told him he had heard the name in a song and thought it sounded unique. One afternoon, using his iphone, Caesar texted Luath and asked if he could join him on a bike ride? Luath replied saying that he had to do some work on the farm but he would be finished in two hours. Caesar confirmed saying, "C U then."

It was a great day to go biking. It was sunny and there was a gentle breeze to help keep them cool. Luath's bike, which he had bought second hand, wasn't as fancy as Caesar's but they both wore the same safety helmets.

"Where are we going?" Luath asked.

"How about up to the dam?" Caesar said.

"Oh that's a long way."

"You can't do it?"

"Yeah, I can be there before you." Luath pushed down on his bike's pedals and gravel shot out behind the rear wheel. "Catch me if you can," he called over his shoulder.

"No problem," shouted Caesar and the chase was on.

It was uphill all the way to the dam. Not a steep hill but definitely without any sections to rest. The first part of the trail was a gravel road and the boys raced along, confident they wouldn't have to look out for any cars or tractors. There was a stone wall alongside the road and when Luath skidded to a halt it was beside a gate in the wall. Quickly he jumped off the bike, pushed the gate open and went into a field. He tried to close the gate before Caesar arrived but he barged through, leaving Luath to secure the gate. Caesar was now in the lead going as fast as he could across a track in a grassy field, with Luath in hot pursuit. Rabbits sprang up from the grass and scampered away and Caesar should have thought about the rabbit burrows but he didn't. He looked over his shoulder to see if Luath was near and at the same instant his front wheel twisted when it caught in a rabbit hole. Caesar flew over his handlebars and landed on the ground with a thump. Luath slowed to see if his friend was okay, and when he saw him starting to get back on his bike he knew it was time to get going. At the far side of the field there was a forest. It was one of the new plantations, where all the trees were planted in straight rows. A path led around the outside but Luath got off his bike and lifted it over a barbed wire fence meant to keep people out. He wasn't the first to have done this; there was an unofficial trail made by other mountain bikers that went through the trees.

Caesar caught up with Luath and the two of them went almost side-by-side, with branches from some trees whipping their faces and legs. Still they pushed as fast as they could because they knew that just ahead there was a stream with a single felled tree over it to provide a crossing. The boys jostled for the lead. They could now see the stream, and neither boy was backing off. With a final surge Caesar's front wheel edged ahead of Luath and with reckless courage Caesar bounced straight on to the log. Luath swerved and fell off his bike. Caesar concentrated on keeping his bike on the log and when he got to the other side he stopped and laughed. Luath knew it was going to be almost impossible to catch Caesar now, but an idea started in his head. Carefully he crossed the log and cycled hard to close the gap with Caesar as much as possible. They had to climb another fence to leave the forest and then ride a track to the dam. Caesar was on his way down this when Luath was just over the fence. He knew it was a little crazy but he had seen other boys doing it and instead of following Caesar, Luath cycled straight to the edge of a rocky embankment that surrounded the dam. Luath crossed his fingers and started bump-jumping his bike down the rocks one jump at a time. He could see Caesar on the path in the distance. Straight down the rocks Luath came and with each successful jump he became more confident. Now Caesar could see what Luath was doing. He knew that if Luath didn't fall there was no way he could beat him to the dam. Caesar stopped and watched Luath make the last two jumps and he was down at the dam. Caesar waved

 and applauded then slowly cycled up to join Luath, who was lying on the grass. Caesar got off his bike and lay down near Luath. They were both sweating and panting hard. Eventually they sat up and drank some water from their bottles.

"That was really crazy to come down those rocks," Caesar said.

"Yeah, I don't know what got into me but I'm glad I'm here in one piece. It was really scary," Luath said.

"I can't imagine what my uncle Christopher would have said if I did that. He lives such a safe life in the big mansion house. It must be really different for you, Luath. My uncle has a lot of people doing all the hard work for him. He has a cook, gardeners and can you believe he doesn't even have to drive his car? He has a chauffeur," Caesar said.

"Well that's certainly different from our home," Luath said. "My father works hard each day. If he is not ploughing fields, then he cuts stones in the quarry for

building walls around the farmers' fields.
He gets just enough money to pay the
farm rent, food, clothes and necessities
for our family.

One time when my father was sick
and couldn't go to work, I heard my mother tell him that
we wouldn't have much money left to buy food once
they paid the rent to your uncle. But they managed with
help from friends till he got well again. You know,
normally our family is happy and content. Whatever
plain food my mother makes must be good for us because
my brothers are strong and my sisters are really clever."

"I bet my uncle Christopher would be surprised to
know that. The people that come to the mansion house
are very snobby and avoid being with working people –
almost like you and I would stay away from doing
homework. Some of the people that work for my uncle
are terrible hypocrites. I was sitting in the room one day
when a man who collected rents from the farmers was
talking to him. Oh, he ranted and called such names of

the farmers who couldn't pay. I think it must be terrible to be a working man," Caesar said.

Luath smiled. "Well if money was the only thing that made life fun you might be right, but most working people I know don't mind doing their job. It lets them get the things they really need. Usually they've worked so hard, sometimes just getting a rest feels like a luxury.

"Trust me Caesar, you don't need lots of money to have fun. You should come to our house at Halloween. We all get dressed up and have parties with singing  and dancing. We go trick or treating and get lots of sweets and fruit. When the children come to our house they have to dunk for apples or they have to try and take a bite from a swinging scone that my mother baked and dripped in treacle. It's great fun. You should be able to hear, at your mansion house, the noise my sisters make when they squeal and my brothers' shout and cheer.

"Or another good time at our house is New Year's Day. It's usually cold and my father needs to keep the fire blazing to make sure the house is warm and inviting. As evening comes, groups of friends and neighbours come around, and each brings part of the meal and then we all sit down to a grand dinner. After, when our stomachs are full, my grandparents sit by the fire talking and joking while we run around the house, playing games. Even the dog joins in barking. Later the adults start dancing and singing. I really love these nights."

"We have parties at our house but there isn't any singing or dancing. My uncle's friends come dressed very fashionably and spend the night just talking and eating dinner," Caesar said. "If children come we're usually sent to the entertainment room in the basement to watch movies or play video games. Like you I really enjoy New Year. My uncle is a good skier and he takes me to Aviemore to ski."

" I don't think my parents could ever afford that. Your uncle and his friends must be really happy with all the money they have," said Luath.

"I'm not so sure. They never have to worry about being hungry or cold. But our house is full of security systems. Floodlights and cameras cover the outside and in the house all the doors and windows have alarms so this must be a worry for them. They spend an awful lot of time discussing how to invest the money they have. When things they can't control go wrong this seems to cause them lots of anguish. Not everyone is like this, but unfortunately lots of them are," Caesar said.

They had made a late start since Luath had to work on the farm and now the sun was starting to set. Fortunately, they knew there would be a long twilight period before it got dark. Buzzing bees made their last flight back to their hives and cows settled down on the grass. Caesar and Luath got up and on to their bikes. "Downhill all the way," they said and took off in the same headlong dash. When they reached the gravel track they waved goodbye and went their separate ways home.

Two Mountain Bikers

William ♥ Nancy

From Robert Burns' poem

When Wild War's Deadly Blast

"When wild war's deadly blast was blawn,

And gentle Peace returning."

William's tour of duty in Afghanistan, with the Black Watch regiment, was finished and he was going home tomorrow. The war continued but already improvements on the way the people lived had been won. Girls were able to return to school again and women were being allowed to be their teachers. Boys and girls were able to safely play in areas, which had been cleared of landmines. William knew peace was not coming cheaply to Afghanistan. There were lots of homes where the children would grow up without a father and the women would have to live as widows.

The next day William was at the airport with his kitbag on his shoulder, waiting to fly home to Scotland. As the plane soared into the sky, he looked out the window at the rows of army tents in which he'd stayed. Beyond them lay the flat, dusty desert and barren mountains. He was glad to be heading home.

A soldier today has a
very tough job to do. It was
not sufficient on this
assignment to be loyal,

brave and fighting to defend the people of Afghanistan.
The army personnel here also had to work hard to
improve the local people's lives. William was proud that
he and his fellow soldiers had helped to build dams for
water conservation, which was then distributed to the arid
land to grow new crops.

When the plane reached its cruising altitude it
levelled out and William slumped back in his chair and
slept. He dreamt of the lush green farm land of Ayrshire
and the river Coil, and of a girl called Nancy that he had
met there. Oh, she probably had met another man while
he was away and wouldn't remember him, he thought.
But he could remember her and her magical smile that
made his heart skip a beat.

"Wake up," said his buddy, "we're home."

William shook his head and looked out the
window and this time he recognised the fertile farmland

around Prestwick airport. All the soldiers went to a base camp, where they spent a week being checked to make sure they were fit. Then at last they were issued passes to return to their homes. William went to the bus depot and boarded the bus to Kilmarnock. When it was just outside the village of Mauchline, he asked the driver to let him off so he could walk to his  family's home. What a blissful change it was to be walking through green fields, past some woods and down the glen where, as a boy, he'd played. His heart beat a bit faster as he recognised the old mill building where he used to meet Nancy when they went out together. He couldn't believe his luck when he came around a corner of the path and there she was outside her mother's house, working in the garden.

William's heart leapt and the emotion was so strong that he turned away quickly to hide tears of happiness that welled up in his eyes.

He gave a good blow of his nose on his white hanky, then dabbing his eyes; he took a deep breath and turned around. Nancy had her head down working with the plants and hadn't noticed him.

He cleared his throat and altered his voice to disguise himself and said,

"Excuse me, I've still got a distance to travel and I'm looking for a bed and breakfast for tonight. But I have to be honest with you I don't have much money; I've just come back from being overseas with the army." Nancy looked up at him and William thought that, with her warm smile, she was even lovelier than the blossoms on the hawthorn hedge around the garden.

At last she spoke. "I had a boyfriend who joined the army, I loved him dearly and I'll never forget him. I can see you're wearing the same uniform, so you're more than welcome to be our guest tonight."

The evening sun had been low in the sky and when she looked at William she couldn't make out his features.

But now she shielded her eyes and stared at him. William saw the colour in her cheeks rise to a pretty rose red colour and then drain away, and she went pale as a pure white lily. She leapt to her feet and rushed up to him and threw her arms around his neck. "William; is that really you?" She cried.

There was no more need for his disguised voice. He could be himself, happy in Nancy's embrace. "Thank goodness I've finished my time in Afghanistan and I have come home," he said. But this homecoming was better than any of his hopes, to find she still remembered and loved him.

Nancy stepped back from him and said, "I didn't think I was going to see you again. You stopped answering my emails. What happened?"

"There were some bad times and some of our unit were killed and I simply couldn't write. I was not sure what each day would bring."

"William; I'm so glad you are home safely," she said.

51

"Maybe I should wait a bit, but I want you to know how much I love you," William said. He reached in his pocket and pulled out a small box and handed it to her. When she opened it there was a small, golden engagement ring and she smiled.

William told her he had saved most of his pay and while he didn't have a lot of money, he wanted to get married to her.

"William while you were away my grandfather retired and he left me a wee farm that is well set up. Yes, we can be married and it will become our home to share.

I've always loved you and hoped so much you'd come back to me," she said.

William put his arms around her and lifted her with a gentle ease that left her heart and feet swinging in the air when they kissed.

He knew that when he chose to be a soldier it wouldn't make him rich like people who worked in the city. What he had earned was a pride in serving his country as only a soldier can. But now it was his turn to start working with Nancy on her farm and raise a family in this safe country, which respected everybody's rights.

The Original Poems by Robert Burns

Following are the original Burns Poems shown in bold print.

(To ease the understanding of Burns' words each line has an interpretation shown in italics)

Caledonia

1

There was on a time, but old Time was then young,
(There was a time long ago)
That brave Caledonia, the chief of her line,
(That brave Caledonia, the chief of her heritage)
From some of your northern deities sprung
(From some of the northern parts came)
(Who knows not that brave Caledonia's divine?)
(Who doesn't know that brave Caledonia is divine?)
From Tweed to the Orcades was her domain,
(From the river Tweed to the Orkneys was her domain,)
To hunt or to pasture, or do what she would.
(To hunt or to farm, or do whatever you choose)
Her heav'nly relations there fixed her reign,
(The gods had blessed this place)
And pledged her their godheads to warrant it good.
(And made sure there was plenty for all)

2

A lambkin in peace but a lion in war,
(A quiet place in peacetimes but a lion in war)
The pride of her kindred the heroine grew.
(The pride of her people the motherland grew)
Her grandsire, old Odin, triumphantly swore:
(Her old god Odin, triumphantly swore)
"Whoe'er shall provoke thee, th' encounter shall rue!"
(Who ever provoke you the encounter shall rue!)

With tillage or pasture at times she would sport,
(With ploughed fields or grasslands at different times
you'd see the countryside)
To feed her fair flocks by her green rustling corn;
(To let sheep graze alongside fields of green rustling
corn)
But chiefly the woods were her fav'rite resort,
(But mainly the forests were the favourite place)
Her darling amusement the hounds and the horn.
(The preferred amusement hunting with hounds and
horn)

3

Long quiet she reign'd, till thitherward steers
(Long quiet she reigned, until this direction comes)
A flight of bold eagles from Adria's strand.
(Roman soldiers from Europe)
Repeated, successive, for many long years,
(Repeatedly over many years)
They darken'd the air, and they plunder'd the land.
(They set fire to the cottages and plundered the land)
Their pounces were murder, and horror their cry;
(They swept in murdering and terrified people)
They'd conquer'd and ravag'd a world beside.
(They'd conquered and ravaged all over the world)
She took to her hills, and her arrows let fly-
(The Caledonians took to the hills and fired arrows at the
Romans)
The daring invaders, they fled or they died!
(The daring invaders they fled or they died!)

4

The Cameleon savage disturb'd her repose,
(The Pict warriors challenged them)
With tumult, disquiet, rebellion, and strife.
(With raids, rebellion and fights)
Provok'd beyond bearing, at last she arose,
(Provoked beyond endurance at last they responded)
And robbed him at once of his hopes and his life.
(And defeated the Picts once and for all and killed some)

The Anglian Lion, the terror of France,
(The English the terror of France)
Oft prowling, ensanguin'd the Tweed's silver flood,
(Often crossing the river Tweed's flood plain)
But, taught by the bright Caledonian lance,
(But experiencing the clever Scottish tactics)
He learned to fear in his own native wood
(The English learned to fear the Scott's attacks from the forests)

5

The fell Harpy-Raven took wing from the north,
(The Vikings came from the north)
The scourge of the seas, and the dread of the shore;
(They were the scourge of the seas and terror of the coastal towns)
The wild Scandinavian Boar issued forth
(The wild Scandinavian army charged out)
To wanton in carnage and wallow in gore;
(To indiscriminate carnage and revel in battles)

O're countries and kingdoms their fury prevail'd,
(Over countries and kingdoms their fury prevailed)
No art could appease them, no arms could repel;
(No art could appease them, no arms could repel)
But brave Caledonia in vain they assail'd,
(But brave Scotland in vain they assailed)
As Largs well can witness, and Luncartie tell.
(As the battles at Largs and Luncartie showed)
6
Thus bold, independent, unconquer'd and free,
(Thus bold, independent, unconquered and free)

Her bright course of glory for ever shall run,
(Her bright course of glory for ever shall run)
For brave Caledonia immortal must be,
(For brave Scotland immortal must be)
I'll prove it from Euclid as clear as the sun;
(I'll prove it from Euclid as clear as the sun)
Rectangle-triangle, the figure we'll chuse;
(Rectangle-triangle, the figure we'll choose)
The upright is Chance, and old Time is the base,
(The upright is Chance, and old Time is the base)
But brave Caedonia's the hypothenuse;
(But brave Scotland is the hypotenuse)
Then ergo, she'll match them, and match them always!
(Then ergo, she'll match them, and match them always!)

Tam O'Shanter

When chapman billies leave the street,
(*When people who are pedlars leave the street*)
And drouthy neebors neebors meet;
(*And thirsty neighbours, neighbours meet*)
As market-days are wearing late,
(*As market-days are getting late*)
An' folk begin to tak the gate;
(*And folk begin to take the road home*)
While we sit bousing at the nappy,
(*While we sit drinking at the bar*)
An' getting fou and unco happy,
(*And getting full and very happy*)
We think na on the lang Scots miles,
(*We think not on the long Scots miles*)
The mosses, waters, slaps, and styles,
(*The bogs, puddles, broken walls and stiles*)
That lie between us and our hame,
(*That lie between us and our home*)
Whare sits our sulky, sullen dame,
(*Where sits our sulky, sullen wife,*)
Gathering her brows like gathering storm
(*Frowning her brow like a gathering storm*)
Nursing her wrath to keep it warm.
(*Nursing her wrath to keep it warm*)
This truth fand honest Tam o' Shanter,
(*This was the situation with honest Tam o' Shanter*)

As he frae Ayr ae night did canter:
(*As he from Ayr one night did ride his horse*)

59

(Auld Ayr, wham ne'er a town surpasses,
(Old Ayr, which is the very best place)
For honest men and bonnie lasses.)
(For honest men and bonnie lasses)

O Tam, had'st thou but been sae wise,
(O Tam, had you but been so wise,)
As taen thy ain wife Kate's advice!
(As taken your own wife Kate's advice!)
She tauld thee weel thou was a skellum,
(She told you often you were a reckless person)
A blethering, blustering, druken bellum;
(A chattering, boasting, intoxicated story teller)
That frae November till October,
(That from November until October,)
Ae market-day thou was nae sober;
(Each market-day you was not sober;)
That ilka melder wi' the miller,
(That after working with the miller)
Thou sat as lang as thou had siller;
(You sat as long as you had money)
That ev'ry naig was ca'd a shoe on,
(That every horse was shod a shoe on)
The smith and thee gat roaring fou on;
(The blacksmith and you got roaring intoxicated)
That at the Lords house, even on Sunday,
(That at the church even on Sunday)

Thou drank wi Kirkton Jean till Monday.
(You partied with Kirkton Jean till Monday)

She prophesied, that, late or soon,
(His wife told him sooner or later)

Thou would be found deep drown'd in Doon,
(He'd be found drowned in *the river Doon*)
Or catch'd wi' warlocks in the mirk
(*Or caught with warlocks in the dark*)
By Alloway's auld, haunted kirk.
(By Alloway's old haunted church.)

Ah! Gentle dames, it gars me greet,
(*Ah! Gentle ladies it makes me weep*)
To think how monie counsels sweet,
*(To think how many co*unsels sweet,)
How monie lengthen'd sage advices
(How many long wise advices)
The husband frae the wife despises!
(The husband from the wife despises!)

But to our tale:- Ae market-night,
(But to our tale: One market-night)
Tam had got planted unco right,
(Tam had got seated very comfortably)
Fast by an ingle, bleezing finely,
(Fast by a fireplace blazing finely)
Wi' reaming swats, that drank divinely;
(*With foaming new ale that drank divinely*;)

And at his elbow, Souter Johnie,
(And at his elbow, Cobbler Johnie,)

His ancient trusty, drouthy cronie:
(*His ancient trusty, thirsty friend*)
Tam lo'ed him like a very brither;
(*Tam loved him like a very brother*)

They had been fou for weeks thegither.
(*They had been drinking for weeks together*)
The night drave on wi' sangs and clatter;
(*The night dragged on with songs and noise*)

And ay the ale was growing better:
(*And always the ale was growing better*)
The landlady and Tam grew gracious
(*The landlady and Tam became friendly*)
Wi' secret favours, sweet and precious:
(*With special favours sweet and precious*)
The Souter tauld his queerest stories;
(*The cobbler told his queerest stories*;)
The landlord's laugh was ready chorus:
(*The landlord's laugh was quick to join in*)
The storm without might rair and rustle,
(*The storm outside might roar and rustle,*)
Tam did na mind the storm a whistle.
(*Tom did not mind the storm at all.*)
Care, mad to see a man sae happy
(*Problems mad to see a man so happy*)
E'en drown'd himself amang the nappy.
(*Even drowned himself among the ale*)

As bees flee hame wi'lades o' treasure,
(*As bees fly home with loads of treasure*)

The minutes wing'd their way wi' pleasure:
(The minutes winged their way with pleasure)
Kings may be blest but Tam was glorious,
(Kings may think themselves blest but Tam felt glorious)
O're a' the ills o' life victorious!
(Over all the problems of life victorious!)
But pleasures are like poppies spread:
(But pleasures are like poppies spread)
You seize the flow'r its bloom is shed;
(You seize the flower its bloom is shed)
Or like snow falls in the river,
(Or like snow falls in the river)
A moment white- then melts for ever;
(A moment white- then melts for ever)
Or like the Borealis, race,
(Or like the Borealis, race)
That flit ere you can point their place;
(That flit before you can point to their place)
Or like the rainbow's lovely form
(Or like the rainbow's lovely form)
Evanishing amid the storm.
(Disappearing during the storm)

Nae man can tether time or tide;
(No man can hold back time or tide;)
The hour approaches Tam maun ride:
(The hour approaches Tam must ride)
That hour, o' night's black arch the key-stane,
(That hour, of night's black arch the key-stone)
That dreary hour Tam mounts his beast in;
(That late hour Tam gets on his horse)

And sic a night he taks the road in,
(*And on such a night he takes the road*)
As ne'er poor sinner was abroad in.
(*As never a poor sinner would go out in.*)

The wind blew as 'twad blawn ts last;
(*The wind blew as if it had blown its last;*)
The rattling shower rose on the blast;
(*The rattling rain was blown on the wind*)

The speedy gleams the darkness swallow'd;
(*Any signs of light the dark night swallowed*)
Loud, deep, and lang the thunder bellow'd:
(*Loud, deep, and long the thunder bellowed*)
That night, a child might understand,
(*That night even a child might understand*)
The Deil had business on his hand.
(*The Devil had business on his hand.*)

Weel mounted on his grey meare Meg,
(*Well mounted on his grey mare Meg,*)
A better never lifted leg,
(*A better horse never lifted a leg*)
Tam skel;it on thro'dub and mire,
(*Tam rode on through puddles and mud*)

Despising wind, and rain, and fire;
(*Ignoring the wind, and rain and lightning*)
While holding fast his guid blue bonnet,
(*While holding fast his good blue bonnet,*)

Whiles crooning o're some auld Scots sonnet
(*While singing over some old Scots sonnet*)
Whiles glow'ring round wi'prudent **cares,**
(*While looking round with prudent cares*)

Lest bogles catch him unawares:
(Unless goblins catch him unawares)
Kirk-Alloway was drawing nigh,
(The church of Alloway was getting closer)
Whare ghaists and houlets nightly cry.
(*Where ghosts and owls nightly cry.)*

By this time he was cross the ford,
(By this time he was across the river fording point)
Whare in the snaw the chapman smoor'd;
(*Where in the snow the pedlar was smothered*)
And past the birks and meikle stane,
(*And past the birches and big stone*)
Whare drunken Charlie brak's neck-bane;
(*Where intoxicated Charlie broke his neck-bone*)
And thro' the whins, and by the cairn,
(*And through the bushes and by the stone monument*)
Whare hunters fand the murder'd bairn;
(*Where hunters found the murdered child*)

And near the thorn, aboon the well,
(And near the thorn, above the well,)
Whare Mungo's mither hang'd herself.
(*Where Mungo's mother hanged herself*)

Before him Doon pours all his floods;
(In front of him the river Doon pours in flood)
The doubling storm roars thro' the woods;
(The doubling storm roars through the woods;)
The lightnings flash from pole to pole;
(The lightning flashes across the sky)
Near and more near the thunders roll:
(Closer and closer the thunders roll)
When, glimmering thro' the groaning trees,
(When, glimmering through the groaning trees,)
Kirk-Alloway seem'd in a bleeze,
(Church- Alloway seemed in a blaze,)
Thro' ilka bore the beams were glancing,
(Through every gap the beams of light were glancing)
And loud resounded mirth and dancing.
(And loud resounded laughter and dancing)

Inspiring, bold John Barleycorn!
(Inspiring, drinking whiskey)
What dangers thou canst make us scorn!
(What dangers you can make us scorn)
Wi' tippenny, we fear nae evil;
(With beer we fear no evil;)
Wi' usquabae, we'll face the Devil!
(With whiskey we'll face the Devil!)
The swats sae ream'd in Tammie's noddle,
(The thoughts so danced in Tammie's head)
Fair play, he car'd na deils a boddle.
(Fair play he cared no devils a farthing)
But Maggie stood, right sair astonish'd,
(But Maggie stood, right sore astonished,)

Till, by the heel and hand admonish'd,
(Until by digging in his heels and slapping her)
She ventur'd forward on the light;
(She moved forward on the light)

And, wow! Tam saw an unco sight!
(And, wow! Tam saw an incredible sight!)

Warlocks and witches in a dance:
(Warlocks and witches in a dance)
Nae cotillion, brent new frae France,
(Not a dance brought new from France)
But hornpipes, jigs, strathspeys, and reels,
(But hornpipes, jigs, strathspeys, and reels)
Put life and mettle in their heels.
(Put life and mettle in their heels)
A winnock-bunker in the east,
(A window seat in the east,)
There sat Auld Nick, in the shape o' a beast:
(There sat old Nick, in the shape of a beast)
A tousie tyke, black, grim, and large,
(A shaggy rough man, black, grim, and large,)
To gie them music was his charge:
(To give them music was his charge)

He screw'd the pipes and gart them skirl,
(He blew the pipes and made them screech,)
Till roof and rafters a' did dirl.
(Till roof and rafters all did rattle)
Coffins stood round, like open presses,
(Coffins stood around like open cupboards)

67

That shaw'd the dead in their last dresses;
(That showed the dead in their last dresses;)
And by some devilish cantraip sleight,
(And by some devilish magic sleight,)
Each in its cauld hand held a light:
(Each in its cold hand held a light)

By which heroic Tam was able
(By which heroic Tam was able)
To note upon the haly table,
(To note upon the holy table,)
A murderer's banes, in gibbet-airns;
(A murder's bones in irons)

Twa span-lang, wee, unchristen'd bairns;
(Two hand-length, small, un-christened children)
A thief new-cutted frae a rape-
(A thief newly cut from a rope)
Wi' his last gasp his gab did gape;
(With his last gasp his mouth did hang open)
Five tomahawks wi' bluid red-rusted;
(Five tomahawks with blood red-rusted)
Five scimitars wi' murder crusted;
(Five scimitars with murder encrusted ;)
A garter which a babe had strangled;
(A garter which a baby had strangled on)

A knife a father's throat had mangled-
(A knife a father's throat had slit)
Whom his ain son o' life bereft-
(Whom his own son of life bereft)

The grey-hairs yet stack to the heft;
(The grey-hairs yet stuck to the handle)
Wi'mair horrible and awefu',
(With more horrible and awful)
Which even to name wad be unlawfu'.
(Which even to name would be unlawful.)
Three Lawyer's tongues, turned inside out.
(Three lawyer's tongues, turned inside out)
Wi' lies seemed like a beggar's clout;
(With lies seemed like a beggar's hat)
Lay stinking, vile, in every neuk.
(Lay stinking, vile in every crack)

As Tammie glowr'd, amaz'd, and curious,
(As Tammie stared amazed and curious)
The mirth and fun grew fast and furious;
(The laughter and fun grew fast and furious)
The piper loud and louder blew,
(The piper loud and louder blew)
The dancers quick and quicker flew,
(The dancers quick and quicker flew)

They reel'd, they set, they cross'd, they cleekit,
(They reel'd, they set, they crossed, they kicked up their heels)
Till ilka carlin swat and reekit,
(Until every witch sweated and was smelly)
And coost her duddies to the wark,
(And cast her rags to the work)
And linket at it in her sark!
(And tripped at it in her dress)

Now Tam, O Tam! Had they been queens,
(Now Tam, O Tam! Had they'd been beautiful)
A' plump and strapping in their teens!
(All fit and full of energy in their teens!)
Their sarks, instead o' creeshie flannen,
(Their dresses instead of greasy flannel)
Been snaw-white seventeen hunder linen!-
(Been snow-white seventeen hundred linen!)
Thir breeks o' mine, my only pair,
(These trousers of mine, my only pair,)
That ance were plush, o'guid blue hair,
(That once were plush, of good blue hair,)
I wad hae gi'en them off my hurdies
(I would have given them off my hips)
For ae blink o' the bonie burdies!
(For a look of the pretty young women)

But wither'd beldams, auld and sroll,
(But withered balding, old and wise)
Rigwoodie hags wad span a foal,
(Old women who could wean a foal)
Louping aflinging on a crummock,
(Leaping, kicking with a walking stick)
I wonder did na turn thy stomach!
(I wonder did not turn your stomach!)
But Tam kend what was what fu' brawlie:
(But Tam knew what was attractive)
There was ae winsome wench and wawlie,
(There was one choice young woman and she was shapely)

That night enlisted in the core
(That night joining in the party)
Lang after kend on Carrick shore
(Long after remembered on Carrick shore)
(For monie a beast to dead she shot,
(For many a beast she shot dead,)
An' perished monie a bonie boat,
(And perished many a good boat)

And shook baith meikle corn and bear,
(And shook both lots of corn and barley)
And kept the country-side in fear.)
(And kept the country-side in fear)
Her cutty sark, o' Paisley harn,
(Her short skirt of Paisley pattern coarse cloth)
That while a lassie she had worn,
(That while as a wee girl she had worn)
In longitude tho' sorely scanty,
(In length although very short,)

It was her best and she was vauntie.
(It was her best and she was proud)
Ah! Little kend thy reverend grannie,
(Ah! Little knew thy reverend grandmother,)
That sark she coft for her wee Nannie,
(That skirt she bought for her wee Nannie,)
Wi' twa pund Scots ('twas a' her riches),
(With two pounds Scots that was all her money)
Wad ever grac'd a dance of witches!
(Would ever have graced a dance of witches!)

But here my Muse her wing maun cour,
(But here my tale speed must increase)
Sic flights as far beyond her power:
(Such flights as far beyond her power)
To sing how Nannie lap and flang
(To sing how Nannie leaped and kicked)
(A souple jad she as and strang);
(A supple woman she was strong)
And how Tam stood like ane bewitch'd,
(And how Tam stood like one bewitched,)
And thought his very een enrich'd;
(And thought his very eye enriched)
Even Satan glowr'd and fidg'd fu' fain,
(Even Satan stared and fidgeted full of admiration)
And hotch'd and blew wi' might and main;
(And jerked and blew with might and force)
Till first ae caper, syne anither,
(Till firstly one caper then another)
Tam tint his rason a' thegither,
(Tam lost his reason all together)

And roars out: "Weel done, Cutty-sark!"
(And roars out: Well done, short skirt)
And in an instant all was dark;
(And in an instant all was dark)
And scarcely had he Maggie rallied,
(And scarcely had he Maggie rallied)

When out the hellish legion sallied.
(When out the hellish legion sallied)

As bees bizz out wi' angry fyke,
(As bees buzz out with angry fear)

When plundering herds assail their byke;
(When plundering herds assail their hive)
As open pussie's mortal foes,
(As wild cats mortal foes,)
When, pop! She starts before their nose;
(When, pop! She starts before their nose)
As eager runs the market-crowd,
(As eager runs the market-crowd)
When "Catch the thief!" resounds aloud:
(When "Catch the thief!" resounds aloud)
So Maggie runs, the witches follow,
(So Maggie runs and the witches follow)
Wi' moni an eldritch skriech and hollo.
(With many an unearthly screech and holler)

Ah, Tam! Ah, Tam! Thou'll get thy fairing!
(Ah, Tam! Ah Tam! You'll get what's coming to you)
In hell they'll roast thee like a herrin!
(In hell they'll roast you like a herring!)
In vain thy Kate awaits thy comin!
(In vain his Kate awaits his coming!)
Kate will soon be a woefu' woman!
(Kate will soon be a woeful woman!)
Now, do thy speedy utmost, Meg,
(Now, do your very speediest Meg)
And win the key-stane of the brig;
(And win the key-stone of the bridge;)

There, at them thou thy tail may toss,
(There, at them you may toss your tail)
A running stream they dare na cross!
(A running stream they dare not cross!)

But ere the key-stane she could make,
(But before the key-stone she could make)
The fient a tail she had to shake;
(The devil following she had to shake;)
For Nannie, far before the rest,
(For Nannie, far in front of the rest)
Hard upon noble Maggie prest,
(Close behind noble Maggie pressed)
And flew at Tam wi' furious ettle;
(And flew at Tam with furious aim)
But little wist she Maggie's mettle!
(But little realized she Maggie's mettle!)
Ae spring brought off her master hale,
(One spring brought off her master whole)
But left behind her ain grey tail:
(But left behind her own grey tail)
The carlin claught her by the rump,
(The witch caught her by the rump)
And left poor Maggie scarce a stump.
(And left poor Maggie scarcely a stump)
Now wha this tale o' truth shall read,
(Now whoever this tale of truth shall read,)

Ilk man, and mother's son, take heed:
(Every man, and mother's son, take heed)

Whene'er to drink you are inclin'd,
(Whenever to drink you are inclined,)
Or cutty sarks run in your mind,
(Or short skirts run in your mind,)
Think! Ye may buy the joys o're dear:
(Think! These joys may cost you dearly)
Remember Tam o' Shanter's meare.
(Remember Tam o' Shanter's mare)

The Twa Dogs

'Twas in that place o' Scotland's isle
(It was in that place of Scotland's isle)
That bears the name of auld King Coil,
(That bears the name of old King Coil,)
Upon a bonie day in June,
(Upon a lovely day in June,)
When wearing thro' the afternoon,
(When wearing through the afternoon)
Twa dogs, that were na thrang at hame,
(Two dogs, that were not often at home)
Forgathered ance upon a time.
(Met once upon a time)

The first I'll name, they ca'd him Caesar,
(The first I'll name, they called him Caesar,)
Was keepit for "His Honour's" pleasure:
(Was kept for "His Honour's pleasure)
His hair, his size, his mouth, his lugs,
(His hair, his size, his mouth, his ears)
Shew'd he was nane o' Scotland's dogs;
(Showed he was not one of Scotland's dogs;)
But whalpit sume place far abroad,
(But a pup brought form someplace far abroad)
Whare sailors gang to fish for cod.
(Where sailors go to fish for cod)

His locked, letter'd braw brass collar
(His buckled, lettered, grand brass collar)

Shew'd him the gentleman an' scholar;
(Showed him the gentleman and scholar)

But tho' he was o' high degree,
(But although he was of high degree,)

The fient a pride, nae pride had he;
(The opposite of pride, no pride had he)
But wad hae spent an hour caressin,
(But would have spent an hour being patted)
Ev'n wi' a tinkler-gipsy's messin;
(Even with a mongrel playing)
At kirk or market, mill or smiddie,
(At church or market, mill or blacksmiths)
Nae tawted tyke, tho'e'er sae duddie,
(No unkempt dog though ever so ragged,)
But he wad stan't, as glad to see him,
(But he would stand as glad to see him,)
An' stroan't on stanes an' hillocks wi' him.
(And chase over rocks and hillocks with him)

The tither was a ploughman's collie,
(The other one was a ploughman's collie,)
A rhyming, ranting, raving billie,
(A rhyming, ranting, raving lively one)
Wha for his friend an' comrade had him,
(Who for his friend and pal had him,)
And in his freaks had Luath ca'd him,
(And his owner in silliness had called him Luath)
After some dog in Highland sang,
(After some dog in a Highland song)

Was made lang syne-- Lord knows how lang.
(Was made long ago – Lord knows how long)
He was a gash an' faithfu' tyke,
(He was a smart and faithful dog)
As ever lap a sheugh or dyke.
(As ever jumped over a ditch or stone wall)
His honest, sonsie, baws'nt face
(His honest plain, pleasant face)

Ay gat him friends in ilka place;
(Always got him friends in every place)
His breast was white, his tousie back
(His breast was white, his shaggy back)

Weel clad wi' coat o' glossy black;
(Well covered with a coat of glossy black;)
His gawsie tail, wi' upward curl,
(His happy tail, with upward curl)
Hung owre his hurdies wi' a swirl.
(Hung over his hips with a swirl)
Nae doubt but they were fain o' ither,
(No doubt but they liked each other)

And unco pack an' thick thegither;
(An unusual pack and close together)
Wi' social nose whyles snuff'd an' snowkit;
(With social nose they sniffed and rummaged)

Whyles mise an' moudieworts they howkit;
(While mice and moles they dug for)

Whyles scour'd awa' in lang excursion,
(*While running away in a long excursion*)
An' worry'd ither in diversion;
(*And worried not with any distraction*)
Till tir'd at last wi monie a farce,
(*Until tired at last with many a silly game,*)
They sat them down upon their arse,
(*They sat them down upon their bottoms*)
An' there began a lang digression
(*And there began a long discussion*)
About the 'lords o' the creation.'
(*About the "Lords of the creation.:*)

CAESAR
I've aften wonder'd, honest Luath,
(*I've often wondered, honest Luath*)
What sort o' life poor dogs like you have;
(*What sort of life poor dogs like you have*)
An' when the gentry's life I say.
(*And when I see the way gentry live.*)
What way poor bodies liv'd ava.
(*I wonder how poor bodies lived at all*)

Our laird gets in his racked rents,
(*Our laird gets his rents paid in goods*)
His coals, his kain, an'a' his stents:
(*His coals, his roof thatch, and all his dues*)
He rises when he likes himself;
(*He gets up in the morning when it suits him*)
His flunkies answer at the bell;
(*His servants answer at the bell*)

He ca's his coach; he ca's his horse;
(He calls his coach; he calls his horse)
He draws a bonie silken purse,
(He carries a fine silken purse,)

As lang's my tail, whare, thro' the steeks,
(As long as my tail, where through the stiches)

The yellow letter'd Geordie keeks.
(The yellow stamped guinea looks)
Frae morn to e'en it's nought but toiling,
(From morning to evening it's nothing but toiling)
At baking, roasting, frying, boiling;
(At baking, roasting, frying, boiling)
An' tho' the gentry first are stechin,
(And even though the gentry eat first)
Yet ev'n the ha' fold fill their pechan
(Yet even servants to fill their stomach)
Wi' sauce, ragouts, an sic like trashtrie,
(With sauce, ragouts and such like rubbish)
That's little short o' downright wastrie:
(That's little short of downright waste)
Our whipper-in,wee, blastid wonner,
(Our whippet dog wee strange thing)
Poor, worthless elf, it eats a dinner,
(Poor, worthless elf, it eats a dinner,)

Better than onie tenant-man
(Better than any tenant-man)
His Honor has in a' the lan';
(His Honor has in all the land)

An' what poor cot-folk pit their painch in,
(And what poor cottage farmers put in their stomach)
I own it's past my comprehension.
(It's past my comprehension)

LUATH
Trowth, Caesar, whyles they're fash't enough:
(Sometimes Caesar, while they're troubled enough)
A cotter howkin in a sheugh,
(A farmer digging in a ditch)

Wi' dirty stanes biggin a dyke,
(With dirty stones as big as a wall)
Baring a quarry, an' sic like;
(Building a quarry, and such like;)
Himsel, a wife, he thus sustains,
(Himself, a wife, he thus sustains)
A smytrie o' wee duddie weans,
(A litter of small wild children)
An' nought but his han'drag to keep
(And nothing but his hand labour to keep)
Them right an' tight in thack an' rape.
(Them right with a roof and rope)
An' when they meet wi' sair disasters,
(And when they meet with miserable disasters)
Like loss o' health or want o' masters,
(Like getting sick or out of work,)
Ye maist wad think, a wee touch langer,
(You would have to think, a little bit longer)
An they maun starve o' cauld and hunger:
(And they must starve of cold and hunger)

But how it comes, I never kend yet,
(But how it comes, I never knew yet,)
They're maistly wonderfu' contented;
(They're mostly wonderfully contented)
An buirdly chiels, an' clever hizzies,
(And *strong sons and clever daughters*)
Are bred in sic a way as this is.
(Are bred in such a way as this is.)

CAESAR
But then to see how ye're negleckit,
(But then to see how you're neglected)
How huff'd an' cuff'd, an' disrespeckit!
(How shouted at and cuffed and disrespected)
Lord man, our gentry care as little
(You know, our gentry care so little)
For delvers, ditchers, an'sic cattle;
(For diggers, ditchers and such farmers;)
They gang as saucy by poor folk,
(They ignore poor folk,)
As I wad by a stinking brock.
(As I would by a stinking badger)
I've notic'd, on our laird's court-day,
(I've noticed, when our lairds sitting at the courts)
(An monie a time my heart's been wae),
(And many a time my heart's been sad)
Poor tenant bodies, scant o' cash,
(Poor tenant bodies, short of cash,)
How they maun thole a factor's snash:
(How they have to endure a factor's abuse)

He'll stamp an threaten, curse an' swear
(He'll stamp and threaten, rant and swear)
He'll apprehend them, poind their gear;
(He'll apprehend them, seize their money;)
While they maun staun', wi' aspect humble,
(While they must stand with aspect humble,)
An' hear it a', an' fear an' tremble!
(And hear it all and fear and tremble!)
I see how folk live that hae riches;
(I see how folk live that have riches;)
But surely poor-folk maun be wretches!
(But surely poor-folk must be wretches!)
LUATH
They're nae sae wretched's ane wad think:
(They're not as wretched as one would think)
Tho' constantly on poortith's brink,
(Although constantly on poverty's brink)

They're sae accostom'd wi' the sight,
(They're so accustomed with the sight,)
The view o't gies them little fright.
(The view of it gives them little fright.)

Then chance an' fortune are sae guided,
(Then chance and fortune are so guided,)
They're ay in less or mair provided;
(They're always in less or more provided)
An' tho' fatigu'd wi' close employment,
(And although fatigued with constant work)
A blink o' rest's a sweet enjoyment.
(A blink of rest is a sweet enjoyment.)

83

The dearest comfort o' their lives,
(The dearest comfort of their lives,)
Their grushie weans an' faithfu' wives;
(Their growing children and faithful wives)
The prattling things are just their pride,
(These happy things are just their pride,)
That sweetens a' their fire-side.
(That sweetens all their fire-side.)

An' whyles twalpennie worth o' nappy
(And while two penny's worth of beer)
Can mak the bodies unco happy:
(Can make the bodies very happy)
They lay aside their private cares,
(They forget their private cares,)
To mind the Kirk and State affairs;
(To think of church and government affairs)
They'll talk o' patronage an ' priests,
(They'll talk of patronage and priests,)
Wi' kindling fury I' their breasts,
(With fire in their hearts)

Or tell what new taxation's comin,
(Or talk about what new taxation is coming)

An ferlie at the folk in Lon'on.
(And marvel at the folk in London)
As bleak-fac'd Hallowmass returns,
(As bleak-faced Halloween returns)
They get the jovial, ranting kirns,
(They get happy with music and dancing)

When rural life, of ev'ry station,
(When rural life, of every class,)
Unite in common recreation;
(Get together for the same kind of fun;)
Love blinks, Wit slaps, an'social Mirth
(Love blinks, with glances and social Mirth)
Forget there's Care upo' the earth.
(Forget there's Care upon the earth.)
That merry day the year begins,
(The Happy New Year day starts,)
They bar the door on frosty win's;
(They bar the door on frosty winds)
The nappy reeks wi' mantling ream,
(The kitchen smells with cooking)

An' sheds a heart-inspiring steam;
(And makes mouth-watering odours)
The luntin pipe, an' sneeshin mill,
(The smoking pipe, and snuff-box)
Are handed round wi' right guid will;
(Are handed round with right good will)
The cantie auld folks crackin crouse,
(The chattering old folks cracking jokes)
The young anes ranting thro' the house—
(The young ones romping through the house)
My heart has been sae fain to see them,
(My heart has been so happy to see them)
That I for joy hae barkit wi' them.
(That I for joy have barked with them)
Still it's owre true that ye hae said
(Still it's too true that you have said)

Sic game is now owre aften play'd;
(This game is now over often played)
There's monie a creditable stock
(There's many a creditable stock)
O' decent, honest, fawsont folk,
(Of decent, honest, hard-working folk,)
Are riven out baith root an' branch,
(Are driven out both house and home)
Some rascal's pridefu' greed to quench,
(By some devious person's greed to have every last penny,)
Wha thinks to knit himself the faster
(Who thinks to tie himself closer)
In favor wi' some gentle master,
(In favour with some gentle master,)
Wha aiblins thrang a parliamentin'
(Where capable ones gather at parliament)
For Britain's guid his saul indentin'
(For Britain's good his soul indenture)

CAESAR
Haith lad, ye little ken about it:
(Listen lad, you little know about it)
For Britain's guid! Guid faith! I doubt it.
(For Britain's good! Good faith! I doubt it.)
Say rather, gaun as Premiers lead him:
(Say rather, following as Premiers lead him)
An' saying aye or no's they bid him:
(And saying yes or no as they tell him.)
At operas an' plays parading,
(At operas and plays parading,)

Mortgaging, gambling, masquerading:
(Mortgaging, gambling, masquerading;)
Or maybe, in a frolic daft,
(Or maybe in the spur of the moment)
To Hague or Calais taks a waft,
(To Hague or Calais takes a trip)
To mak a tour an' tak a whirl,
(To make a tour and take a whirl,)
To learn bon ton, an' see the worl'.
(To learn bon ton, and see the world)
There, at Vienna or Versailles,
(There, at Vienna or Versailles,)
He rives his father's auld entails;
(He uses his father's old inheritance)
Or by Madrid he taks the rout,
(Or by Madrid he takes the route)
To thrum guitars an' fecht wi' nowt;
(To strum guitars and fight with nobody)
Or down Italian vista startles,
(Or to Italy on a visit starts)
Hunting amang groves o' myrtles
(Hunting among groves of myrtles)
Then bowses drumlie German-water,
(Then sits in muddy German-water,)
To mak himself look fair an' fatter,
(To make himself look fair and fatter,)

An' purge the bitter ga's an' cankers
(And purge the bitter talk and skin soars)
O' crust Venetian bores an, chancers.
(Of old Venetian bores and people.)

For Britain's guid! For her destruction!
(For Britain's good! For her destruction!)
Wi' dissipation, feud an' faction.
(With squandering, fighting and arguing.)

LUATH
Hech man! Dear sirs! Is that the gate
(Oh no man! Dear sirs! Is that the way)
The waste sae monie a braw estate!
(The waste of so many a good estate!)
Are we sae foughten an harass'd
(Are we so troubled and harassed)
For gear ta gang that gate at last?
(For wealth to go that way at last?)

O would they stay aback frae courts,
(O would they stay away from courts,)
An please themsels wi' countra sports,
(And please themselves with country sports,)

It wad for ev'ry ane be better,
(It would for everyone be better,)
The laird, the tenant, an' the cotter!
(The laird, the tenant, and the farmer!)
For thae frank, rantin, ramblin billies,
(For those free roistering young men)
Fient haet o' them's ill-hearted fellows;
(Devil take all of them ill-hearted fellows)

Except for breakin o' their trimmer,
(For wasting their inheritance)
Or speakin lightly o' their limmer
(Or speaking lightly of their mistress)
Or shootin of a hare or moor-cock,
(Or shooting of a hare or moor-cock,)
The ne'er-a-bit they're ill to poor folk.
(They're unkind and they're ill to poor folk)

But will ye tell me, master Caesar:
(But will ye tell me, master Caesar;)
Sure great folk's life's a life o' pleasure?
(Are rich people's life's a life of pleasure?)
Nae caluld nor hunger e'er can steer them,
(No cold nor hunger ever can steer them)

The vera thought o't need na fear them.
(The very thought of it need not fear them.)

CAESAR
Lord, man, were ye but whyles whare I am,
(Lord, man, were you but staying where I am,)

The gentles, ye was ne'er envy em!
(The gentlemen, you would never envy them!)

It's true, they need na starve or sweat,
(It's true, they need not starve or sweat,)
Thro' winter's cauld, or simmer's heat;
(Through winter's cold, or summer's heat;)

They've nae sair wark to craze their banes,
(They've no hard work to craze their bones)
An' fill auld-age wi' grips an' granes:
(And fill old age with gripes and groans)
But human bodies are sic fools,
(But human bodies are such fools,)
For a' their colleges an' schools,
(For in spite of all their going to college and schools,)

That when nae real ills perplex them,
(That when no real ills perplex them,)
They mak enow themsels to vex them;
(They make enough themselves to vex them;)
An' ay less they hae to strut them,
(And if less they have to show them,)
In like proportion, less will hurt them.
(In the same way, less will hurt them.)

A countra fellow at the pleugh,
(A country fellow at the plough)
A countra girl at her wheel,
(A country girl at her wheel,)
Her dizzen's done, she's unco weel;
(Her dozen bobbins of wool done she's very happy)
But gentlemen, an' ladies warst,
(But gentlemen, and ladies worse)

Wi' ev'n down want o' wark are curst:
(With even not having to work are cursed)
They loiter, lounging, lank an' lazy;
(They sit around, lounging, doing nothing;)

Tho' deil-haet ails them, yet uneasy:
(Although devil-has it nothing's wrong with them, yet they're uneasy)

Their days insipid, dull an' tasteless;
(Their days insipid, dull and tasteless;)

Their nights unquiet, lang an' restless.
(Their nights noisy, long and restless.)
An' ev'n their sports, their balls an' races,
(And even their sports, their balls and races,)
Their galloping through public places,
(Their rushing through public places,)
There's sic parade, sic pomp an' art,
(There's such parade, such pomp and art,)
The joy can scarcely reach the heart.
(The joy can scarcely reach the heart.)

The men cast out in party-matches,
(The men dressed up in fancy clothes,)
Then sowther a' in deep debauches;
(Then join all in deep debauches;)
Ae night they're mad wi' drink an' courtin',
(Each night they're mad with drink and chasing girls)
Niest day their life is past enduring.
(Next day their life is past enduring.)

The ladies arm-in-arm in clusters,
(The ladies arm in arm in clusters,)
As great an' gracious a' as sisters;
(As great and gracious all as sisters;)

But hear their absent thoughts o' ither,
(But hear their absent thoughts of the other)
They're a'run deils an' jads thegither.
(They're all run devils and angels together.)
Whyles, owre the wee bit cup an' platie,
(While over the little bit cup of tea and small scone)
They sip the scandal-potion pretty;
(They enjoy the tales of scandal)

Or lee-lang nights, wi' crabbit leuks
(Or live-long nights, with complaining looks)

Pore owre the devil's pictur'd beuks;
(Pour over the devil's picture books)
Stake on a chance a farmer's stackyard
(Bet on a chance a farmer's crop)
An' cheat like onie unhang'd blackguard.
(And cheat like any unhanged blackguard.)

There's some exceptions, man an' woman;
(There are some exceptions, man and woman)
But this is Gentry's life in common.
(But this is typical of gentry's life.)

By this, the sun was out o' sight,
(By this time the sun had set,)
An darker gloamin brought the night;
(And twilight came before the night)
The bum-clock humm'd wi' lazy drone;
(The beetle hummed with lazy drone)

The kye stood rowtin' I' the loan;
(*The cattle stood lowing in the field*)

When up they gat, an' shook their lugs,
(*When up they got and shook their ears*)
Rejoic'd they were na men, but dogs;
(*Rejoiced they were not men, but dogs*)
An' each took aff his several way
(*And each took off his different way*)
Resolv'd to meet some ither day.
(*Resolved to meet some other day.*)

When Wild War's Deadly Blast

1

When wild war's deadly blast was blawn,
(When wild war's deadly blast was over,)
And gentle Peace returning,
(And gentle Peace returning,)
Wi' monie a sweet babe fatherless
(With many a sweet babe fatherless)
And monie a widow mourning,
(And many a widow mourning,)
I left the lines and tented field,
(I left the lines and tented field,)
Where lang I'd been a lodger,
(Where long I'd been a lodger,)
My humble knapsack a'my wealth,
(My humble knapsack all my wealth,)
A poor and honest sodger.
(A poor and honest soldier)

2

A leal, light heart was in my breast,
(A loyal, light heart was in my breast,)
And for fair Scotia, hame again,
(And for fair Scotia, home again,)
I cheery on did wander:
(I happily on did wander)

I thought upon the banks o' Coil,
(I thought about the banks of the river Coil,)

I thought upon my Nancy,
(I thought about my Nancy,)
And ay I mind't the witching smile
(And always I remembered the magical smile)
That caught my youthful fancy.
(That captured my youthful fancy.)

3

At length I reach'd the bonie glen,
(At length I reached the lovely glen,)
Where early life I sported,
(Where when I was young I played,)
I pass'd the mill and trysting thorn,
(I passed the mill and the thorn tree we met at,)
Where Nancy aft I courted.
(Where Nancy often I courted.)
Wha spied I but my ain dear maid,
(Who spied I but my own dear maid)
Down by her mother's dwelling,
(Beside her mother's house,)
And turn'd me round to hide the flood
(And I turned around to hide the flood)
That in my een was swelling!
(That in my eye was swelling!)

4

Wi' altered voice, quoth I:-- "Sweet lass,
(With altered voice, said I, "Sweet lass,)
Sweet as yon hawthorn's blossom,
(Sweet as that hawthorn's blossom,)
O, happy, happy may he be,
(O, happy, happy may he be,)

That's dearest to thy bosom!
(That's dearest to your heart!)
My purse is light, I've far to gang,
(My purse does not have much money in it, I've far to go)
And fain would be thy lodger;
(And I would like to be your lodger)
I've serv'd my king and country lang
(I've served my king and country long)
Take pity on a sodger.
(Take pity on a soldier)

5

Sae wistfully she gaz'd on me,
(So wistfully she gazed on me,)
And lovelier was than ever.
(And lovelier was than ever.)
Ouo' she:-- "A sodger ance I lo'ed
(Said she, "A soldier once I loved)
Forget him shall I never.
(I'll never forget him.)
Our humble cot, and hamely fare,
(Our humble spare bed, and homely fare,)
Ye freely shall partake it;
(You can stay as our guest)
That gallant badge – the dear cockade
(That gallant badge and regimental colours)
Ye're welcome for the sake o't
(You're welcome because of them)

6

She gaz'd, she redden'd like a rose,
(She gazed, she reddened like a rose,)

Syne, pale like onie lily,
(Then went pale like any lily)

She sank within my arms, and cried:
(She collapsed within my arms, and cried)
"Art thou my ain dear Willie?"
("Art you my own dear Willie?")
"By Him who made yon sun and sky,
(By Him who made the sun and sky,)
By whom true love's regarded,
(By whom true love's regarded,)
I am the man! And thus may still
(I am the man! And thus may still)
True lovers be rewarded!
(True lovers be rewarded!)

7

The wars are o'er and I'm come hame,
(The wars are over and I'm come home,)
And find thee still true- hearted.
(And find you still true-hearted.)
Tho'poor in gear, we're rich in love,
(Although poor in money, we're rich in love,)
And mair, we'se ne'er be parted.
(And more we'll never be parted)
Quo' she:-- "My grandsire left me gowd,
(Said she, "My grandfather left me gold,)

A mailen plenish'd fairly!
(A farm provided fairly!)

And come, my faithfu' sodger lad,
(And come, my faithful soldier lad,)
Thou'rt welcome to it dearly!
(You're welcome to it dearly!)

8

For gold the merchant ploughs the main,
(For gold the merchant sails the seas,)
The farmer ploughs the manor;
(The farmer ploughs the manor fields)
But glory is the soger's prize,
(But glory is the soldier's prize,)
The sodger's wealth is honor!
(The soldier's wealth is honor!)
The brave poor sodger ne'er despise,
(The brave poor soldier never despise)
Nor count him as a stranger:
(Nor consider him as a stranger)
Remember he's his country's stay
(Remember he's his country's strength)
In day and hour of danger.
(In days and hours of danger.)

The Original Poems by Robert Burns

Author's Note

Welcome to the back of the book. I'm assuming you've read the book and are looking for more. There are two more "Introducing Mr. B." books. The stories were grouped with subjects to suit different age groups and with your completion of the Battle collection this is the most mature. If you have not read the, **"The Friends Collection,"** I believe you would also derive pleasure out of it. In these stories;

Fiona calls Alan on Skype for help with her homework assignment – Andrew's grandfather takes on Google – Gordon heads up a school project to save a river drying up – Hamish and Lorna go to the cinema.

In the first book, **"The Farmer Collection,"** the stories are probably too simplistic for you but the Burns poetry and the interpretations should still be of interest. The poems included are; To a Louse, To a Mouse, Poor Maillie's Elegy, and The Auld Farmer's New Year Salutation to his Auld Mare Maggie.

Acknowledgements.

I have been fortunate to have the support of several people in writing the book. Firstly there was my friend Ian Robertson. He has spent his career as an elementary school teacher, vice principal and principal. An enrichment of the stories came about as a result of the considerable time he took to evaluate the content. A major point he suggested was the stories were not uniform in being suitable for all age groups. This led to breaking the twelve stories I had written into three groups of four.

I approached the Vancouver Burns Club to ask if some of their members would read and comment on the books. At this stage the books were comprised of the stories and the original Burns poems. Both reviewers from the Burns Club, Andrew Sanderson and Capt. Donald Sinclair were very encouraging. One major recommendation I received from them was, "That if I was including the original poems I should include a glossary with them." I worked at that but found it cumbersome. In the end I decided that since I was endeavouring to reach younger readers that providing a line by line interpretation of the poems would be most effective.

One other person was Mandy Thomson, who is a primary school teacher in Scotland. She confirmed that there was a variation on suitability of the stories for different age groups.

Last but not least, as always, the support of my wife Pamela.

The Author.

Norman Strathearn Thomson P Eng

I was born in Perth, Scotland and schooled in Glasgow. At the age of twenty three I emigrated to Canada, where I have spent my adult life raising a family and working. But absence does make the heart grow fonder. Throughout the years I have organized Burns suppers for the Rotary Club, attended Burns Suppers at the Seaforth Highlanders of Canada and participated in Burns suppers at friends homes. Perhaps Burns is in my genes as my grandfather was the president of the Glasgow Bridgeton Burns Club 1934/35. During many trips to Scotland I have visited the Burns Cottage and the spectacular New Burns Museum at Alloway.

The Illustrator

Nicholas Lennox

I was born in Glasgow Scotland but raised in Fife. I have a degree in Animation and Electronic Media. My carreer todate has let me work on a variety of film and television shows, which included the Oscar nominated film "L" Illusioniste' (2010) and the Disney XD show "Randy Cunningham: 9th Grade Ninja (2013). I currently live and work in Dublin Ireland where I continue to both animate and illustrate.

CPSIA information can be obtained
at www.ICGtesting.com
Printed in the USA
FSOW03n1550240715
9035FS